The Brothers Grimm
The Twelve Princesses

Retold by Oakley Graham   Illustrated by Natalie Smillie

Licensed exclusively to Top That Publishing Ltd
Tide Mill Way, Woodbridge, Suffolk, IP12 1AP, UK
www.topthatpublishing.com
Copyright © 2016 Tide Mill Media
All rights reserved
2 4 6 8 9 7 5 3
Manufactured in China

ISBN 978-1-78445-591-0

A catalogue record for this book is available from the British Library

There was once a king who had twelve beautiful daughters. They slept in twelve beds all in one room, and when they went to bed the door was locked.

However, every morning their shoes were full of holes from dancing all night! Nobody could find out how it happened, and the princesses refused to tell the king where they had been each night.

The king did **NOT** like the princesses keeping secrets from him!

So he made an announcement and promised that if any person could find out where the princesses went at night, he would make them the richest person in the entire kingdom.

If they tried and failed, they would be thrown into the castle dungeons!

Soon, a brave knight arrived at the palace. When evening came, he was taken to the bedroom next to the princesses'.

The knight's plan was to stay awake all night and keep watch to see if he could discover their secret.

But the knight soon fell asleep; and when he awoke in the
morning the princesses' shoes were full of holes from dancing all night.

The king was **angry** that the knight had failed to find out the princesses'
secret, and the poor knight was thrown into the castle dungeon.

After the knight, many others tried to discover the princesses'
secret; but they all had the same luck, and were also imprisoned.

An old soldier heard about the king's promise.

On his way to the palace he met an old woman, who asked him where he was going.

'I am on my way to see the king to find out where the princesses go to dance at night,' he said.

'Well,' said the old woman, 'take care not to drink the wine which one of the princesses will bring to you; and as soon as she leaves, pretend to be fast asleep.'

Then she gave the old soldier a cloak and said, 'This cloak will make you invisible, and you will be able to follow the princesses wherever they go.'

Filled with hope, the old soldier went to see the king, and when evening came he was led to the bedroom next to the princesses'.

As the clock struck midnight, the eldest princess brought the old soldier a cup of wine; but he threw it away secretly, just as the old lady had told him to. Then he lay down and pretended to fall asleep. But as soon as the princess left the room, he put on his special cloak and followed her.

In the princesses' room, the twelve princesses took out all their fine clothes, and dressed themselves ready for dancing.

... zzzzzzzzz

But the youngest princess was worried.
'I don't know why, but I feel very uneasy tonight,' she said.

'You are always afraid,' said the eldest princess. 'Have you forgotten how many people have already tried to find out our secret and failed?'

Then the eldest princess clapped her hands three times and a secret trapdoor flew open!

Amazed, the old soldier watched the princesses going down through the trapdoor, and then, as quick as a wink, he followed them.

However, in the middle of the stairs he stepped on the dress of the youngest princess. 'Someone stepped on my dress!' she screamed to her sisters.

'You silly thing!' said the eldest.
'You must have caught it on a nail in the wall.'

At the bottom of the stairs there was a magical wood; and the trees had leaves that were silver and gold.

The old soldier wanted some proof for the king, so he broke off a little golden branch.

The youngest princess heard the branch snapping.
'Something is not right – did you hear that noise?' she whispered.

But the eldest princess said, 'It is only our princes,
who are shouting with happiness at our approach.'

The princesses went on until they came
to a lake where there were twelve little boats
with twelve handsome princes in them.

Each of the princesses climbed into a boat, and
the old soldier got into the same boat as the youngest.

On the other side of the
lake stood a magical castle.

Inside the castle, the old soldier watched as the twelve princesses danced until the sun was about to rise and their shoes were worn out.

Then the princes rowed them back over the lake and the princesses promised to come again the next night.

In the morning, the old soldier was taken to the king. The king asked him, 'Where do my daughters go to dance at night?'

The old soldier answered, 'With twelve princes in a magical castle.'

Then the old soldier told the king everything that had happened, and showed him the golden branch which he had brought back with him as proof.

The king called for the princesses, and asked them if the old soldier was telling the truth. The princesses could not lie to the king now that their secret had been discovered, so they confessed.

Just as the king had promised, the old soldier was rewarded with riches beyond his wildest dreams. The king was so happy that he released all of the prisoners from the castle dungeons too.

And as for the magical castle? Sadly, the spell was broken, and the twelve princesses never saw or danced with their princes again.